Sarah & Duck

go to the
FUNFAIR

Sarah and Duck are heading to the park. They've had a busy day and are looking forward to relaxing on their favourite bench.

Oh, what's this?
The park looks different.

WOW! Look at all the colours!

says Sarah.

Well I never . . . it's a **fairground!**

Oh, isn't that Scarf Lady over there?
Maybe she knows where your bench is.
Why don't you go and ask her . . . ?

Go on, Duck. Throw the hoop over a toy and you'll win it.

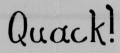

Well done, Duck! Now you can collect your prize.

Hey, I'm not a prize!

Quack!

says Duck.

Sarah, didn't you have something to ask Scarf Lady?

Oh yes. Have you seen our bench, Scarf Lady?

asks Sarah.

Bench . . . hmmm . . . Oh yes, I have seen it! It was near something . . . rooounnnd . . .

says Scarf Lady.

But hello – what's this?
It's a carousel!

Oooh!
It's round!
Quick, Duck!

says Sarah.

Quack!

says Duck.

Maybe you'll be able to spot the bench as the carousel goes round? On you hop!

Come on, Duck! Quick!

says Sarah.

Quack!

Can you see your bench yet?

Hmm, not yet . . .

To help us find our bench.

says Sarah.

Well, I'm on my way to work and that Ferris wheel looks like the biggest, roundest thing here. Why not join me?

Whenever I'm up in the sky, I can see everything quite clearly.

says Moon.

That sounds like a great idea.

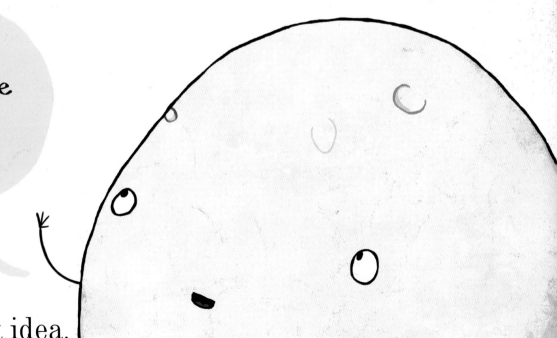

Fasten your seatbelts, Sarah and Duck.

Click!

Click!

Oops!

Click!

Ah, there you go, Moon.

Up you go.
Can you see your bench yet, Sarah and Duck?

Um, no.
Not yet.

says Sarah.

Duck! Look, our bench!

says Sarah.

Quack!

You've found it! **Well done!**

Come on, you two. Let's go and say hello to your bench.

Hello, bench.

says Sarah.

Quaaack.

says Duck.

Now, isn't that quite the view.

The End